ARTHUR'S
Honey Bear

An I Can Read
Picture Book™

ARTHUR'S
Honey Bear

Story and Pictures by
Lillian Hoban

BARNES & NOBLE BOOKS
NEW YORK

Barnes & Noble Publishing, Inc.
122 Fifth Avenue
New York, NY 10011

ISBN 0-7607-6501-4
Printed and bound in the United States of America
05 06 07 08 09 MCH 10 9 8 7 6 5 4 3 2 1

For Eban and Willa Hagerty

It was spring-cleaning day. Violet was cleaning out her toy chest. She made two piles of toys. One to keep, and one to put away.

Arthur was sticking stamps into his stamp album.

"I am going to clean out my toy chest too,"
said Arthur. "And I am going to have a Tag Sale."
"What is a Tag Sale?" asked Violet.

"A Tag Sale is when you sell your old junk," said Arthur.

"I don't have any old junk," said Violet. "I want to keep all of my toys."

"When I was little," said Arthur, "I wanted to keep all of my toys too. But now I want to sell some of them."

Arthur began to clean out his toy chest.

He took a pile of toys to the back steps.

Arthur took his Hula-Hoop, his Yo-Yo, a pile of finger paintings, and his china horse.

He took his Noah's Ark, his baby King Kong, his sand-box set, his Old Maid cards, and his rocks and marbles.

Then he took out his Honey Bear.

"Father gave me Honey Bear when I had the chicken pox," said Arthur. "Honey Bear always tasted my medicine for me when I was sick."

Arthur moved Honey Bear behind baby King Kong.

"Now I will make the price tags," said Arthur.

"Let me help," said Violet.

"You can cut the paper for the tags," said Arthur, "and I will write the prices."

Arthur made a big sign.
It said:

Then Arthur marked the prices on the tags. He put tags on all the toys and pictures and rocks and marbles.

"You didn't put a tag on Honey Bear," said Violet.

"He is in very good shape," said Arthur. "He has only one eye missing. Maybe I should sell him for a lot of money. Maybe I should sell him for thirty-one cents," said Arthur.

"His ear is raggedy," said Violet.

"Well," said Arthur, "I have not made up my mind yet."

He moved Honey Bear all the way behind baby King Kong.

"Now," said Arthur, "we have to make arrows.
Then everyone will know where the sale is."

Violet cut arrow shapes out of paper. Arthur
wrote "Tag Sale" on them.

Arthur and Violet hung the arrows on trees.

"Now we will wait for someone to come and buy,"
said Arthur.

They waited and waited. They had some cupcakes and milk. Violet had a chocolate cupcake with white frosting, and Arthur had one with pink frosting.

Then Norman rode up on his bike.

"How much are the cupcakes?" he asked. "I have three cents."

"The cupcakes are not for sale," said Arthur.
"But the rocks are three cents. So are some of
the pictures."

Norman looked at all of the rocks. "I don't see any I want," he said.

Then he tried the Yo-Yo. "It doesn't snap up," he said. "Who wants to pay eleven cents for a Yo-Yo that doesn't yo-yo?"

He picked up the Old Maid cards. "Only babies play Old Maid," said Norman.

"I play Old Maid," said Violet, "and I am not a baby anymore."

"This is not a good sale," said Norman. "My old toys are better."

He got on his bike and rode away.

"Here comes Wilma," said Violet. "Maybe she
will buy something."

"Tomorrow is my sister's birthday," said Wilma. "Do you have anything good?"

"Well," said Arthur, "here is a very nice Hula-Hoop."

"It's bent," said Wilma. "And my sister *has* a Hula-Hoop."

"Here is a china horse," said Arthur.

"How much is the bear?" asked Wilma.

"What bear?" asked Arthur.

"The bear behind baby King Kong," said Wilma. "He doesn't have a price tag."

"Oh," said Arthur quickly, "he costs a lot."

"Well, how much?" asked Wilma.

"Your sister won't like him," said Arthur. "She is too old for stuffed toys."

"No she isn't," said Wilma. "She takes her stuffed pig to bed with her."

"Well," said Arthur, "I will sell him to you for fifty cents."

"All right," said Wilma. She took fifty cents out of her pocket.

"Do you gift wrap?" asked Wilma.

"No," said Arthur.

"Well," said Wilma, "I don't have money for gift-wrap paper. If I buy a present at the toy store, they will gift wrap for nothing."

Wilma put the fifty cents back in her pocket and walked away.

Arthur looked at Honey Bear and hugged him.

He held Honey Bear and ate the rest of his cupcake.

"I wish someone would buy *something*,"
said Arthur.

Violet said, "I will buy something, Arthur.
I will buy your Honey Bear."

"You don't have any money," said Arthur.

"I have thirty-one cents," said Violet. "I can give you thirty-one cents and my brand-new Color-Me-Nice coloring book. None of the pictures are colored in yet."

"Well, maybe," said Arthur. "But maybe I want to keep Honey Bear for myself."

"I thought you said you don't want to keep your old junk," said Violet.

"Honey Bear is not old junk," said Arthur. "He is my special bear."

"I will give you thirty-one cents, my Color-Me-Nice coloring book, and my box of crayons," said Violet. "Only the purple one is broken."

"Honey Bear has been my bear for a long time," said Arthur. "He wants me to take care of him."

"I will give you thirty-one cents, my coloring book, my crayons, and half a box of Cracker Jack with the prize still in it," said Violet.

"Well, all right," said Arthur.

So Violet gave Arthur thirty-one cents, her crayons, her coloring book, and half a box of Cracker Jack.

Arthur gave Violet his Honey Bear.

Arthur took all of his sale things and put
them away.

He put the thirty-one cents in his mail-box bank.
He ate some of the Cracker Jack.

He read the fortune on the prize wrapper. The fortune said: "Someone you love is gone." A ring was inside. Arthur put it on.

Then he colored a picture in his Color-Me-Nice coloring book. He colored a picture of a boy holding a teddy bear.

Violet came in holding Honey Bear. He was dressed in a pink tutu. He was wearing a necklace and a bonnet.

"Honey Bear is a *boy*!" said Arthur. "He does not like those clothes."

"Honey Bear is my bear now," said Violet. "I will dress him the way I want."

"You don't know how to take care of him," said Arthur.

"Well, I am his mother now," said Violet, "and I am taking care of him."

"I think Honey Bear misses me," said Arthur. "He wishes he were still *my* bear."

"Well, he's not," said Violet. She took Honey Bear for a walk.

Arthur sat down and ate some more Cracker Jack. He took the ring, and put it on a different finger. He opened the Color-Me-Nice coloring book again.

Then he whistled a little tune, and thought for a while.

Violet came back. She sat down with Honey Bear.

Arthur thought some more.

Then he said to Violet, "Violet, are you
my little sister?"

"Yes," said Violet.

"Well then, do you know what I am?" said Arthur.

"You are my big brother," said Violet.

"Yes, I am," said Arthur, "and do you know what that means?"

"No," said Violet.

"That means I am Honey Bear's UNCLE!"
said Arthur.

Arthur picked up Honey Bear and hugged him.

"I am your uncle, Honey Bear," said Arthur.

"I will always be your uncle."

"And do you know what uncles do?" said Arthur.

"What do uncles do?" asked Violet.

"Uncles play with their nephews, and they take them out for treats," said Arthur.

"Honey Bear likes treats," said Violet. "Can I
come too?"

"All right," said Arthur.

Arthur took the thirty-one cents out of his
mail-box bank. Then he and Violet walked Honey
Bear to the candy store. Arthur and Violet
and Honey Bear had chocolate ice cream cones.

Honey Bear ate his ice cream cone on his Uncle Arthur's lap.

"Honey Bear, I am glad I will always be your uncle," said Arthur.

Then Violet and Arthur helped Honey Bear eat
all of his ice cream.